The WATERING CAN

Printed in the United States of America
First Printing, 2019
ISBN 9781703712704

Sterling, Ct
www.artistmarnie.com

Dedicated to my family, who supports me in
my dream of being an artist.
Ronnie, R3, Stephanie and Dad.

Thanks to Susan
for always being there for me.

A special thanks to
Rhianna & Everleigh
for being my muses.

Love you more!

There was a young Mom who loved flowers.
And this young Mom had a young daughter
who also loved flowers.

The Mom spent evenings watering the many flowers in her yard, and the young Daughter followed.

The Daughter saw her Mom watering flowers and wanted to water flowers too!

So the Mom and Daughter went to the store and bought a smaller watering can for the little girl.

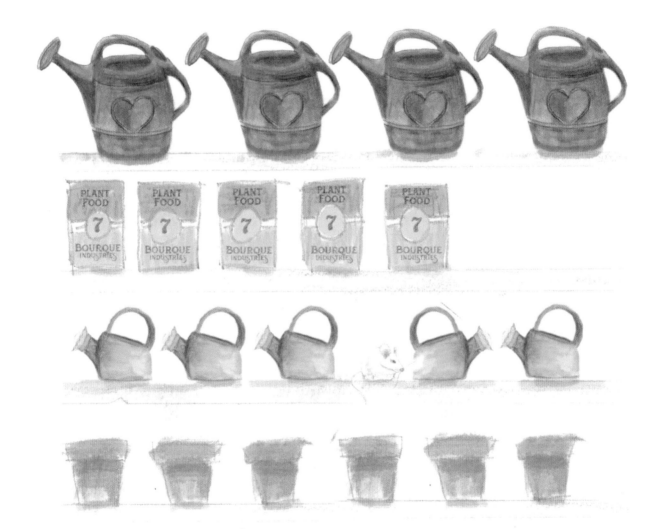

The Mom and Daughter
watered daffodils when
they arrived in spring.

And stargazers that filled the air
with their heavenly scent.

The Mother and Daughter watered irises playing peek-a-boo through the fence.

They watered black eyed susans,

bright pink peonies,

and blue hydrangeas.

The little girl grew, and started
using the Mom's watering can.

Then the little girl grew older still, and it was just the Mom watering the flowers.

And the little
watering can sat...

and sat.

Until one day, another little girl saw
her Mimi watering her flowers and
wanted to water too!

And Mimi was happy to have a
little girl helping again!

Flower Index

Black Eyed Susans

Daffodils

Irises

Hydrangeas

Peonies

Petunias

Roses

Stargazers

Tulips

Miss you Mom!

Marilyn A. Reynolds

1946-2016

If I had a flower for each time I thought of my
Mother, I could walk in my garden forever.
Anonymous

THE END

Marnie is an author, artist, as well as a new Mimi!
She paints daily, and when not painting,
she dreams of traveling with her loved ones.

She has also written another book called "*Cousins*" about the bonds
of family. It has a family tree inside so you can remember loved
ones, and teach your little ones about their family.

Marnie and her supportive hubby Ron, are the parents of two
children and love being Grandparents. Marnie tries to live life being
grateful, rather than sad that her children are grown up and leaving
the nest. That was the inspiration for this book.

artistmarnie.com

Made in the USA
Middletown, DE
12 August 2020